With thanks to the wonderful
hoomans of High Hopes Dog Rescue:
Tara Carr, Drea Hinton, Hayley Cartland, Sam Weston
and D'Arcy Pearce.

Thanks for all you do for our four legged friends

Thanks also to another amazing hooman,
Julie Bentley, for design and layout work.
Your help was above and beyond.

Thanks must also go to Karen Breen, for...well,
everything. xx

WWW.HIGHHOPESDOGRESCUE.ORG

For my family: Nicola, Sam,
Penny (still the best dog ever), Willow...
and of course the one who made this possible in the
first place, Indiana Bones.

3

You got chickie again hooman
  – *Yep*
Want some
  – *No. It's cooked in soy sauce and that's bad for you.*
I'll put my paw on your leg
  – *No*
I'll drool
  – *No*
You know what happen when you dint gimmie chickie.
  – *Yes, you ripped up a tuggy toy*
Yeh... dat is nice guitar over dere
  – *I'll cook you some chickie.*

Dis my happy face
   – *Why? What are you up to?*
Me had chickie and den me bark at
doggie in door
   – *That's your reflection you moron*
Dat me?
   – *Yep.*
Me handsome
   – *Yes, you are.*
Me wag tail. Him wag tail. Him and me
friends now. Fanks for my chickie butler.
   – *I AM NOT YOUR BUTLER!*
Yeh, you is.

1

Hooman..

    – Yes Indy?

Me want a bell

    – Why?

Cat got a bell...

    – Yes, but it's on her collar because she
    goes out into the field and kills things

Me want bell. Me say please

    – Why?

Me can den summon butler to play tuggy

    – I AM NOT YOUR BUTLER!

Yeh, you is.

Hooman!

– Yes Indy

It Christmas day!!

– No, that's next Friday. 7 days to wait buddy.

It today. One day is 7 dog days so it today

– No

Me open dis when you went to kitchen

– Oh for... she's going to be cross with you, it's mummy's.

Nope. She cross wiv you, cos me handsome, and you is just a butler.

– I AM NOT YOUR...nevermind, get the sellotape.

━━

Hooman. HOOMAN! Look at me.

– Indy, I want to go and have a bath...

NO! NO say da B word...

– Sorry... shower.. what do you want now?

Me seen dat film where da big boat can't swim

– Um... you mean Titanic?

Yeh. Dat one.

– Oh... so?

So... dat bestest fing me ever see. Me is Rose now

– Eh?

Me being Rose and you is...

– Please don't say Jack because that'll get so weird.

No... you is just a butler.

– Okaaaay?

Draw me butler. Draw me like one of your French poodles.

– Indy, you're so weird.

Gnight butler

– Goodnight Indy.

13

Hooman!!!!

– *Yes Indy?*

Wot dat?!

– *That's a rainbow.*

Wow. Dat nice.

– *Yes... they're made when sunlight passes..*

Me know song about rainbow. Dog song.

– *OK*

Me sing it you

– *OK*

Grey and grey and grey and grey, grey and grey and grey. Me can sing da rainbow.

– *Let's just look at it shall we?*

Hooman!!!

   – I'm busy Indy.

But dis important.

   – OK what is it? You'd better not think you saw Leonardo DeCaprio again.

No. Me see sumfin spickius

   – You mean suspicious.

Yeh. Dat.

   – What was it?

It black and had pointy ears and it scoping out dat house over dere. It burglar.

   – Indy, that's their cat.

Me call police. Me key witness. Me solve case.

   – Right. You're not watching re-runs of The Bill on Dave any more.

Hooman?

   – Yes Indy?

Wot doin?

   – Wrapping a present. Go back to watching Kylie for a minute.

Who it for?

   – Wait and see.

It for me innit? Lemmie see label. Me read good.

   – Oh... and when did you learn to read?

Me learn when seeing credits for Titanic.

   – Right... OK. Label says I.N.D.Y. know what that spells?

Yeh. Dat spell Leonardo DiCaprio.

   – No it...

Him my favrit. Him best Ninja Turtle too.

   – No buddy it's for you.

What bout cat?

   – No, it's not for her.

Dis best day ever.

Hooman!!

    – Yes Indy?

Be good butler an keep lookout

    – Why?

Me splash in puddle

    – So?

So me see big Rottweiler doggie back dere

    – And?

If him see me splashy, den him make big fun

    – And what's so wrong with that?

Him tell cat. You butler. You do as told OK?

    – OK.

Me splashy

    – Quick he's looking!!

No! Me bark! Me chase him!

    – Hahaha ha!! Got ya, you sucker.

Me get you for dis butler, me get you.

Hooman!!!

– Yes Indy?

You is in trouble now

– Why? What have I done now?

You butler yes?

– Well, not really but...

NO. You is butler. You do buttle stuff

– What's your point?

Me had to get post. Dat butler's job

– Oh God no...

Me got post. Me had to open post all by my own

– Oh Indy, look what you have done!!

Dis wot happen when you not do wot me pay you for

– YOU DON'T PAY ME. I AM NOT YOUR BUTLER!!!

Yeh. You butler. You buttle. You is on probation now.

Hooman‼

    – Yes, Indy. I'm trying to watch Spongebob you know.

Me know. Look at dis. Wot dis?

    – Eh? That's your ball.

Yeh me know. Indy's ball. Whose ball dis?

    – It's your ball Indy.

Dat's right. Not butler's ball. Indy's ball.

    – What's your point buddy?

Me give you ball, so you learn to chuck it me.

    – Actually it's me that throws it so you learn to fetch it.

Ha. Dat wot hooman fink. Hoomans stoopid. Me bring, you chuck.

    – You want me to throw it boy? Here, fetch‼

Good hooman. You is learning.

Hooman!!! HOOMAN!!

   – Yes Indy.

Me need get upatairs

   – What? No. You'll just jump on the beds and try to eat the cat.

Me no eat cat. Forget cat. Me need to get on roof.

   – Erm... why do you want to get on the...

Me need to watch over house like merciless vengeance of da night.

   – Eh?

Me seen Batman. Me Batdog now. You is Alfred da butler. You do Batdog's buttleing. Me need protect house.

   – From whom exactly?

Cat next door and postman.

   – The house is fine Indy and..

BATDOG

   – The house is fine Batdog.

Let me on roof Alfred.

   – Seriously buddy I'm going to hide the TV remote now.

Me Batdog. Me bestest good boy detective.. me find it.

   – No Indy. Go back to watching Kylie.

Hooman...

  – *Yes Indy.*

What mum doin?

  – *Wrapping a present for Sam.*

When Sam here den?

  – *Not until after Christmas, he's with his mum.*

Mum not his mum den?

  – *Well, she's not your mum, or Willow's mum,*
  but she still is really. So yes, she is. We all think
  she is.

Him lucky like me lucky.

  – *Certainly is. You're a lucky doggie Indy.*

Butler?

  – *Yes?*

If me so lucky, why me not have biscuit wot
mum got in tea mug?

  – *Because you stole mine.*

Dat true. Me eat dat so you don't die of beetles.

  – *Diabetes buddy, and I don't have it but*
  thanks.

You is welcome, butler.

Hooman!!

- *Indy I'm trying to watch Star Trek.*

Me know dat. But me got joke. Dog joke.

- *Really. And where did you hear this joke?*

Me make up joke. Me send to floppy head-fur hooman.

- *Floppy head-fur... you mean Michael McIntyre?*

Yeh. Dat him. Dis joke right up his walkie. Me tell butler as treatie.

- *Right. Go on then.*

Ok. Knock knock hooman.

- *Who's there?*

Cat

- *Cat who?*

Ha ha ha!! Cat not knock. Cat got own door. Stoopid hooman!!

- *Is that it?*

Yeh. Dat funny if dog. It da way I smell dem.

- *Just go to bed Indy.*

Hahahahahahahahahahaha! Me funny.

Hooman!!!

    – Yes Indy?

Sparkle hooman howling is on da TV

    – That's Kylie. You like Kylie.

Me do. Me can sing da howling like
sparkle lady.

    – No please don't...

Me just can't get food out me head

    – Stop.

Wow wow woooooooow aaaaooooowwwww

    – Stop it.

Butler, get me sparkle dress.

Me Kylie now.

Hooman!!!! HOOMAN!!!!

 – *Yes Indy?*

Who is you hooman?

 – *Eh?*

What is you in house for. Me not know you.

 – *Indy, it's me!*

Me not know you!! Me bark.

 – *Indy, it's me. I've just put a hat on is all.*

Me chase you. Me get butler. Butler smack nose and put you in your crate and call you bad boy.

 – *Indy... mate it's me.*

BUTLER!!!! BUTLER COME QUICK!!!

 – *Look, I'll take the hat off OK? There.*

Fank good boy dat you is here butler. Dere was a not you hooman here.

 – *No buddy, it was me. I was wearing a hat.*

Me chase him and him gone now.

 – *No I just had a hat on*

Him gone. Me save house and you and mum and cat. Me hero.

 – *OK, there's a good boy. You can have a treaty.*

Me want medal.

 – *Alright then, and a medal.*

35

Hooman!

    – Yes Indy. Can't we just watch Elf now?

No. Me and butler play game.

    – OK.

Dog game. Game called "Wot dis is?"

    – OK. What do I have to do?

Me say movie, book, song and fings like dat.

    – Oh yes, I know it.

Me den say one bark, two bark, free bark and dat

    – Yes. We call it charades.

Yeh. Dat. Butler ready?

    – Yes.

OK. It movie. It one bark.

    – I don't know.

Look at me hooman. Me over here, den me over dere.

    – You're just running about having a zoom.

Nope. Try again butler. Look wot me do.

    – I don't know.

Me near. Me far. Wherever me are.

    – Oh, God it's Titanic isn't it.

Yeh. Dat is it butler. You is good boy.

Hooman!!!

   – Yes, Indy?

Me explore. Look wot me found.

   – Aww. It's a little diddy waterfall in the brook.

Me discover dis. Me explorer now.

   – Well, we have been here before. Yesterday for example.

Yeh. But me not discover dis den. Me only finded dis den.

   – Right... isn't that the same thing?

No. Cos water not same now. Bigger now. Like dat big one on TV.

   – Niagara Falls?

Yeh. Dat one.

   – Oh... if you say so.

Me do. And me got idea.

   – Go on then...

Butler, you go back to house.

   – What for?

Butler get cat size barrel and den get cat.

   – Indy...just... no.

39

Hooman...

   – *Yes, Indy?*

You no see me butler.

   – *Well, I can see you. I can see the top of*
   your head.

No. Me seen Ninja Assassin movie. Me stealth
dog now.

   – *I see.*

No, you no see. Dat whole point. Me train 20
years for dis.

   – *Indy you're only 10 months old.*

Yeh. Dat how good me is. Me one with shadows
and darkness.

   – *Right. And what exactly will you use this*
   new power for?

Me follow cat to bottom of garden. Den Cat
jump into tree. Den me lost cat.

   – *Well, yes. That's how she gets into the field.*

Cat up to sumfin. Cat got knives for fingers... cat
is bad ninja. Me take out cat, quick and painless.

– *Right well I'm going back to sleep.*

Butler get me throwing star and nun-chuks.

– *No, Indy.*

41

Hooman.

– Yes Indy?

Me upset butler. Me upset.

– Why buddy, what's wrong?

Cat. Cat wrong.

– Why, what has she done?

Cat say me look like Dobby.

– Awwww buddy. You're handsome.

Dat wot me said. Cat said me Dobby and me get socks for Christmas.

– And that's upset you because why?

Cos it butler wot is house elf.

– Thanks Indy. Socks it is then.

43

Hooman!! HOOMAN!! Come quick!!!
  - *What's up Indy? I'm trying to pretend I don't have a crush on Ellie from Countryfile.*
Dat not important. Dis is. Wot dis?
  - *Eh? What's what?*
Dis fing. Me go sleep. Me wake up and dis here. Dis new.
  - *Well, that's our new oven. We had to get one after the kitchen flooded.*
Wot it do butler?
  - *It cooks our meals.*
It cook chickie?
  - *Yes we're having Chicken for dinner.*
It cook Moo Chickie?
  - *You mean Beef?*
Yeh, dat.
  - *Yes, it cooks beef.*
Me like. Chickie go in big door.
  - *Yes and there's a little side oven too, which we can use...*
For cat.
  - *No Indy!!*
Yeh. Chickie in big door. Cat in little door.
  - *OK... whenever we go out you're going in your crate.*
Butler, get me cook in sauce.
Me feel like kitty tonight.

Hooman!!

> *– Yes Indy?*

Me stuck Butler. Get me out.

> *– You're not stuck Indy, just walk*
> *backwards.*

Me stuck. Cat went through cat door and
me follow and now me stuck.

> *– You do look funny though.*

Dis not funny, butler. Me not laffin. Cat
say me look like Winnie da Pooh.

> *– OK I'll get the key and open the door.*

Quick, cat gone to get phone and send
piccie to Rottweiler down road.

> *– I'll be just a moment.*

Get me out dis butler and me give you
pay rise.

Hooman.

– *Yes, Indy?*

Come here. But me warn you butler, butler be quiet.

– *Why? What's up?*

Me is keepin lookout.

– *What for?*

Cat.

– *But she's indoors asleep.*

Not all of dem.

– *You're standing guard against all cats...*

Yeh. Me seen dis on Game of Thrones. Me Night's Watch now.

– *Right. Well look, you know that lions and panthers and tigers are all types of cat too?*

Dey is?

– *Yes, and you're going to do what against an army of tigers exactly?*

Me bark and me say grr and dem go away.

– *I think we'll be OK Indy. You coming back inside?*

Butler get me treatie?

– *OK.*

Winter coming butler, winter coming.

Hooman!!

    – Yes Indy...

Butler!! You is back quick!

    – I went to get my coffee from the machine. You OK?

Yeh. Just dat you is back more quicklier dan me fink you would be.

    – Anything you want to tell me Indy?

Nope. Don't fink so. Me good, fanks.

    – So, the sausage that was on my plate... where's that then?

Cat took it.

    – No, she's upstairs asleep.

Cat sleep eatin.

    – No she's not... try again.

Sam eated it. Sam, him come and him eat sossij an den he left.

    – No because he's not here until next week, and that's not now is it?

No... dis is dis week and dat is dat week. Me learn dat.

    – Right, so where is my sausage.

Ted doggie from over da road, him come in and him...

    – Don't tell fibs Indy... you ate it didn't you?

Yeh, me eated it, butler. Me sorry.

    – Right, so are you a good or a bad boy?

Me is good boy cos butler left plate at same height as me and me not want to drool on carpet or mum get cross wiv butler so me save butler by eatin sossij.

Hooman!
- *Indy I'm having a stress. What's up?*
What dis butler. Wot dis on me nice new floor?
- *That's my toast. Dropped on the floor and as always it lands butter side down. That's called sod's law.*
Me like toastie corner.
- *I know.*
Toast ALWAYS land butterdown?
- *Yes*
Ha! Cat always land cat up.
- *Yes that's also true.*
Me got idea. Me got idea for physics spearmint.
- *I think you mean experiment.*
Yeh dat one. Butler, get me toast, cat and sellotape.
- *Why?*
Me sellotape toast to back of cat.
- *Right....why?*
Den me throw cat off roof.
- *What?! Why?*
Me fink dis... me fink cat try to land cat up and toast try to land toast down. So cat spin.
- *Wait... you're saying the the force of sod's law will cancel out natural law and create a new equalibrium whereby the cat lands both upright and upside down, and the toast exists within that paradigm too and will try to land butter side down...so the cat will simply rotate at an accelerating velocity forever, thus proving the reality of Heisenberg's uncertainty principle in conjunction with Boyles laws, and solving the world's energy crisis forever?*
Yeh. Dat.
- *That's not a bad shout Indy...*
An den cat will explode.
- *Oh... well, no then.*

Hooman.

– *Yes Indy?*

How long me have to do dis butler?

– *Do what?*

Well, me finked it good plan to be friend wiv cat.

– *Aww buddy that's brilliant.*

Well, it Christmas. Good willies even to cat.

– *It's just goodwill, but that's nice of you.*

Yeh dat wot me fink. So me find cat...

– *And?*

Me say me an cat play game.

– *Right.. so what are you playing?*

Cat game. It called hide an not find.

– *You mean hide and seek?*

Yeh dat wot me say and cat say no, cat game called hide an not find.

– *I think I'm getting the picture buddy.*

So.. me have to hide and cat count to billion. Me not know what dat is. Me fink it bigger dan ten.

– *Yeah. Just a bit.. look mate...*

An me been here now since dis mornin an me really need a wee now.

– *OK... buddy, the cat was having you on. She went out at lunchtime.*

Cat not find me?

– *Sorry mate... she's not going to, no.*

But dat mean...

– *Yes, I'm afraid so..*

DAT MEAN ME IS WINNER!!!! Me good boy and have treat now butler.

– *Yes... go and do a wee first.*

Yeh. Dat good plan. You is best butler.

Hooman!

   – Yes Indy?

Me need you butler.

   – Oh really? I can't imagine why.

Dis not funny butler. Me is caught in trap.

   – Well you've just wrapped your...

No. Me see squiggle...

   – It's called a squirrel Indy.

Yeh, dat. Me see squiggle and him run. Me chase and him go round and round tree.

   – And you followed.

Yeh an den him ambush me wiv trap.

   – I see. Well look, why not just walk around the tree the other way.

Me dog. Dog not do dat.

   – No... you don't do you?

Hooman!!!

- Yes Indy!!

It Christmas Day before!!

- We call it Christmas Eve Indy.

Yeh. Dat. An look who me found!! Me found Eaorle!

- Well, OK but you're not to chew him.

No, him an me friends. Cat say me an him is muppets.

- Well, he is. You're... you're just special.

Yeh. Me is. Me an Eaorle found control for Disney +

- OK but if you ruin The Mandalorian before Sam gets here, then you'll be in a world of trouble.

No. Me not do dat. Me an Eaorle we watch Muppet Christmas Carol.

- No... wait until Mum gets home tonight.

OK den me watch...

- Die Hard? Lethal Weapon? Ninja Assassin 2?

No me watch best movie ever.

- No. Please not again.

Me watch Titanic.

- Please no.

Get popcorn butler, an me have large diet fizzy pop too.

Hooman.

– Yes Indy?

Me seen movie on Netflix when you was out.

– Oh... what was that then?

Me do actin' an you got to guess butler.

– Indy I'm trying to tidy up after you.

Butler can buttle later. Now butler is guessing movie.

– OK

First me is all nice look

– Yes..

And den me go like dis. Waaaaaaaaaaaaaaah.

– The Thing.

No, not dat. Me not allowed dat in case me copy dat.

– That's true. Give me a clue.

It like spider-hooman, but bad spider-hooman.

– OK... um...

It have dat hooman in wot mum want to lick face.

– Well that's either Hugh Jackman or Tom Hardy.

Yeh. Dat one.

– I know... Venom.

Yeh. Me Venom now.

– But Venom eats people whole.

Yeh. Me know. Cat not know. Cat about to find out.

Hooman?

    – Yes Indy?

Wot dat?

    – I am preparing something for your dinner sir.

Oooh. Butler say sir. Me like dat. Me approve. Wot me having.

    – Well... here you go.

Dog food?

    – Just move it about...

Butler!!! It chickie!!! It chickie butler!!

    – Yes Indy, merry Christmas eve.

Me love you butler. You buttle better dan anyone.

    – Love you too buddy.

You tell cat me say dat an me get you butler, me do poo in butler shoes.

Hooman!!!! Hooman!!! Hooman!!!

   – Yes, Indy?

It Christmas Day!!!!

   – Yes mate, merry Christmas.

Yeh. Waggy Christmas butler. Now.
What me got?

   – You'll have to wait and see mate.
   But you can help mum open these.

Yeh yeh yeh yeh yeh. Me do dat.

   – Right so just..

Me rip everyfin butler.

   – OK just.. calm down a bit eh?

No. Me roll and rip and roll and tear and
me bark and bark and bark

   – Good grief. It's like Sam when he
   drank that Sunny D.

Me do got present though butler.

   – Yes, it's downstairs.

Wot cat got?

   – Right now? More dignity than you.

Hooman.

   – *Yes, Indy*

How many crates till next Christmas butler?

   – *365 buddy, even if you're not using your*
   crate by then.

But dat is...dat is... dat...

   – *2,555 dog crates buddy.*

Me can count to ten. Dat, I fink, is more.

   – *Yes it is... but guess what?*

Wot?

   – *Sam is coming in 3 days' time and we get*
   to do Christmas again because he's my boy
   and I miss him terribly.

Free days is...

   – *21 dog crates Indy.*

Dat nuffin. Me do six of dem now cos me a bit
sleepsy but everyfin smells like good.

   – *OK well you watch Kylie, we'll have*
   Christmas Dinner and then you can have
   some beef with yours.

Me is happily me adopted mum and dat you
my butler, butler.

   – *Us too mate.*

67

Hooman!

- *Yes Indy?*

Butler, wot today?

– *Well, today is Boxing Day Indy.*

Good. Me bet me knockout cat in 2 rounds.

– *No no, not that kind of boxing.*
Traditionally, presents were given on boxing
day, and people opened boxes.

Santa coming back?

– *No buddy, we had our presents yesterday,*
but we saved some for when Sam comes on
Monday. Do you know who Santa is and
what that's all about?

Yeh. Dere is Mary and Jofus and Baby Jeefus.

– *Well, not quite...*

And Santa is Baby Jeefus grandad.

– *OK there's quite a lot wrong with that so...*

An dis is him hat.

– *Yes but...*

Not now butler, you buttle me breakfast now
cos me in training to box cat.

– *Oh, brilliant.*

Hooman!

– Yes Indy?

How many fingers you got butler?

– Um.... what?

In right hand. How many fingers?

– Indy I'm trying to make coffee.

Me know dat. Dis important.

– Isn't it always? Anyway look...

No. Me seen Princess Bride. Me Inigo
Montoya now. You kill father. Prepare to die.

*– Ah.. OK. Look, I am not the six fingered
man... you see? Four fingers and a thumb.*

Dat make six.

– No... that makes five.

Yeh... dat. Me needs to find six fingers man.

– You know what though?

Wot butler?

*– The cat's got an extra finger halfway up
her leg.*

Dat true!!! Hey cat... me name Inigo Montoya.
You kill father. Prepare to die.

Hooman.

 – Yes Indy.

Wot dis movie butler?

 – It's Die Hard. My favourite Christmas film.

Wot Snape doin?

 – That's not Snape. That's Hans Gruber.

 An exceptional thief.

Me know it Snape really. Me like dis. Me John McClane now.

 – Well, OK but don't say it.

Mum gonna be cross wiv you butler. Dis got bad words in it.

 – Shush Indy this is a good bit.

Butler get me a vest and den me throw cat off roof.

 – No Indy.

But look where cat is butler. It just need a little push.

 – No Indy, please just leave her alone.

Me say it...

 – No.

Yippee Kai Ay Mothe...

 – Get in your crate Indy.

Ha. Wen Snape fall off roof, me not see why Snape not just fly broomstick.

 – Great. Well that's Die Hard ruined. Cheers.

73

Hooman!!

   – *Yes Indy?*

Wot dis? Wot going on?

   – *There's been a big storm buddy and that's*
   runoff water coming up out of the drains.

No. Dat boring. We is sinking.

   – *Well, there are a lot of people this morning*
   who have their houses underwater.

Dat like Spongebob!

   – *Erm... no... not quite and it's not funny.*

Spongebob is funny butler, me an butler watch
Spongebob all time.

   – *Yes, but I mean it's not funny that people*
   have lost their possessions and their homes.

Butler can adopt dem. Like me adopted mum.

   – *It's not quite as simple as that mate.*

Anyway, we is sinking.

   – *No. I know where you're going with this and*
     just... don't.

We IS sinking butler and dat means

   – *No. Please God not again...*

Me is near, me is far, whereeeeeeeever me are!!!!
Me Rose, you butler and dis Titanic.

   – *I changed my mind. I'll be Jack. At least*
   he dies.

Me fink me handcuff cat to side of ship.

Hooman!!!

   – Yes Indy?

Look at all dis! You better buttle dis before mum get back butler.

   – What the?! I left the room for 2 minutes and look at the mess!

Me not do dis!

   – Right... don't you dare tell me it was the cat because she's upstairs asleep.

Oh... um... den it was...

   – No, it wasn't Sam because he's not here until tomorrow.

But...dere was... dis massive fing...um...

   – Yes?

Dis flood damage.

   – No it isn't, nothing is wet.

Me can make it wet.

   – No. You don't that in the house and you know it.

Dis woz like dis wen me got here.

   – You better tidy this up or Mum will be so cross.

Yeh. Cross wiv you. Cos me is handsome and you is just butler.

   – I'll get the bin.

Yeh. You do dat an me work on solving mystery of wot did dis. Me bettin on it was bigfoot.

Hooman.

    – Yes, Indy?

Me want to see face butler.

    – Oh, you don't need...

Me do butler. Me see if you still laffin.

    – Me? No. This is my dead straight empathy face.

Me nearly drown butler.

    – No you didn't you idiot, you jumped in a puddle and sank.

Yeh an it went right over head!

    – Yes, well don't jump in puddles when it's flooded then.

Me tell you butler, if me not seen Aquaman, me would not have made it.

    – It was very funny.

Dis not funny butler. Mum dint fink so.

    – Indy. She nearly wet herself laughing.

Me not laffin. Cat say me Vicar Of Dibley. Me not even know wot dat mean!

    – Well the main thing is you're OK. And you've had a bath now too.

No say da B word. Anyway. Dat not main fing.

    – No?

No butler. Main fing is wen you is in da B word later, me throw cat in. See who laffin den butler.

Hooman!!!

 – *Yes Indy?*

Wot dat?!

 – *That's a deer buddy. They live in the woods.*

Wot dey for butler?

 – *What? They're not...*

Dey is for chasin butler.

 – *No.*

Yeh. Me is fastliest good boy zoomin dog.

 – *That's as maybe but no.*

Butler, you like comic books.

 – *Yes, but that's got nothing to do with...*

Me is Flash now.

 – *That's not fair Indy. You know I love*
 The Flash.

Me is Flash butler, butler likes dat...

 – *You'd never catch up with them anyway.*

Yeh me would. Know why?

 – *Why?*

Cos me is Flash.

 – *Come on, let's go home.*

Hooman‼

– Yes Indy?

Wot dat fing?

– Well, Sam's coming for his Christmas and for his birthday too, so we got you this.

Wot is?

– It's an Orang Utan.

Dat is monkey.

– NO‼ IT'S NOT A MONKEY. IT'S AN APE‼

Butler, you is one of dem.

– Yes. Hoomans... I mean, humans, well, yes we are apes.

Dat funny butler. Dat mean you throw poo at cat.

– No, that's not going to happen.

Butler?

– Yes Indy?

Me on Google. Google say dis...."the argument that monkeys and apes are separate in genealogy is quickly eroding amongst scholars. There is little to no evidence that the distinction of a prehensile tail and the absence of such in the classic ape is in any way genetic and simply more of an evolutionary branching of the same species."

Know wot dat mean butler?

– What?

Dat mean me watch Planet of da Monkey later and you not can say nuffin and me laff an laff an laff.

Hooman!

   – Yes Indy?

Me seen Milan now butler

   – Mulan Indy, it was called Mulan.

Yeh dat.

   *– Let me guess. You now need to disguise yourself
as a girl and go and fight the cat.*

Dat not funny butler. Everyone fink me girl anyway.

   *– Not anymore they don't. Everyone knows you're
a boy dog.*

Yeh, dat cos me is boy dog.

   – Yes, just a very pretty one.

Why Mulan have to not be girl hooman?

   *– Well, humans kind of have this thing where the
men did all the fighting and the girls stayed home
and had babies.*

Dat stoopid. Dogs not care if girl or boy dogs.
It not matter.

   *– No and it shouldn't and doesn't, or at least
humans are starting to think that way. With a
little bit of understanding, a bit of luck and some
hope, we may just build a better society where
everyone is seen as having the same value and
mankind can move forward to a better future,
with everyone in harmony.*

Butler, it too early for dat Star Trek rubbish.
It simple. You make food, me chase cat.
Dat all dere is to life.

Hooman!!

– Yes Indy... though I'm not happy with you.

Me seen deer again butler.

– Yes.

And me was off lead when me see dem.

– I know.

And me was good boy.

– Yes, for about 5 seconds.

Yeh den me chase and chase and chase and chase and chase and chase an den me stop. An den me chase and chase and chase and chase and chase and chase and den me stop.

– Yes, and me and Sam had to run after you for ages.

Sam did butler, but you is fat so you did puffinhuffin.

– Yes, thanks for that.

Me did come back wen Sam say so.

– Yes you did.

So me is good boy really butler. Me want bubbly squeak, moo chickie and sossij for breakfast.

– You can have dog food.

Dat good too butler, dat good too.

Hooman.

    – Yes Indy?

Wot dis me is wearin? Wot you done to me butler?

    – It's a thermal coat buddy. It'll keep you warm.

Why cat not got one den?

    – Well, cats have a higher metabolism.

Wot?

    – Metabolism.

Me like dem. Me like Nuffin Else Matter an me like
Enter Sandhooman.

    – No... that's Metallica. Metabolism is how you burn
    your energy.

Yeh, dat. Why it pink butler?

    – Because it was Penny's, but you don't need a coat
    over the rainbow bridge. It's warm there.

So den, it girl coat.

    – Well... the one we bought you was too big.

It girl coat butler. Cat already say me is girl.

    – Well when we get back from Sam's birthday
    breakfast we'll change it.

Dis give me idea though.

    – OK... what's that then?

Me wrap cat in sellotape and say it is spanx.

    – No Indy. Just...no.

Hooman!

    – Yes Indy?

Wot dis butler?

    – It's the hot tub buddy.

It look like da B word. You no say dat.

    – Well it's not a ba..

NO!! NO SAY DA B WORD!!

    – OK... B.A.T.H.

Yeh, dat. Me know wot dat spell.

    – Yes, it spells...

Leonardo Dicaprio.

    – No Indy, you think everything spells that.

Well, him my favrit. Him have licky face.

    – I think he might not see it that way but there you go.

Butler, me pay you to do wot me say yes?

    – Well, not really... but go on.

Butler get cat.

    – Why?

Me want to play Aquacat.

    – No Indy.

Hooman.

    – Yes Indy?

Me is embezzled.

    – I think you mean embarrassed.

Yeh dat.

    – It was funny Indy.

It not funny butler.

    – Well...

Stop laffin.

    – OK... why wasn't it funny?

Me see hedge chickie.

    – You mean a Pheasant

Yeh dat. Me seen him all sittin on icy puddle.

    – Uh-huh, and then what did you do?

Me chase him so me can catch him

    – And...

And him not stuck in icy puddle at all! Him fly off and me go skiddy and slippy.

    – Yep... and then?

An den me stop spinnin and stands up and den ice go snap an me fall in.

    – Pahahahahahahaha!!!!

Dis not funny butler. Me nearly drown.

    – In a puddle.

Yeh.

    – You're such an idiot.

Hooman!!!

    – Yes Indy?

Who is me butler, who is me?

    – What? You're Indy. Stop being a moron.

Ha! Butler not know. No hoomans know who me is.

    – OK I'm lost.

Me do howling and hoomans and butler guess who is me.

    – Oh Christ. You've watched The Masked
    Singer, haven't you?

Yeh. An dis is mask.

    – No you idiot you've just fallen asleep with
    your head in your blanket.

No!! Me do howling...

wooooowowowowowowoooooooowowowow-oooooooo.....

So, who is me den?

    – If I get you some beef will you stop?

Yeh butler, me stop for moo chickie.

    You're not having the control for the telly
    anymore.

Butler?

    – Yes?

Me wuz Betty Boo.

    – Oh, good.

Hooman!!! Hooman!!!
Hoooooooooomaaaaaaannnnnn!!!

– *Yes Indy?*

Butler look at size of dat river chickie!!!

– *It's a Swan. Leave it alone.*

No butler. Me bark an bark an bark an bark an
bark an bark an me say grrrr and den me bark an
bark.

– *And how far did that get you?*

Him say hiss.

– *Exactly.*

Him say hiss lots. Me fink dat is river chickie bad
word.

– *Swans are a bit like Gina Carano. Beautiful to
look at but can easily break every bone in your
body... unlike Gina though, they can be very
grumpy indeed.*

Me leave river chickie alone den.

– *Yes, good plan.*

Me fink cat need to come on walkie.

– *No.*

Cat would love it. All dis fresh air.

– *Indy you are not weaponizing a Swan.*

Yeh... me is.

Hooman!!!

    – Yes Indy?

Who dat, butler?

    – What?

Why is you keepin annuvver doggie in dis cupboard?

    – What are you talking about now?

Dere butler, right dere!! Me see him. Who him?

    – That's your reflection you idiot.

No. It doggie. You keeps him locked up.

    – No mate it's just...

You is a cycle path butler. Me is on to you.

    – I think you mean psychopath and no, it's your reflection.

Me will find dat doggie and me get him.

    – How? How are you this dumb?

Hooman...

– Yes Indy.

Butler... me fink dat you is cross.

– A bit, yes. But not really.

Me said me is sorry butler.

– Yes, but an apology means nothing unless you mean it.

Me does means it butler.

– Prove it then. Tell me what you did.

Well... me wuz on nice walkie in da top fields

– Yes...

An me did runnin an chasin an zoomin...

– Yes...

An...an.. an me see deers an me wuz off lead...

– Yes...

An me came back so me is good boy best boy.

– Yes that was a good boy thing but that's not what you did bad was it.

...no butler. Den me did bad fing.

– What was that then?

Me found sumfin.

– What?

Me found a squeak chickie.

– Yes. You found a mouse didn't you.

Yep. Me found little squeak chickie an den...

– Yes...and then?

Den me ate him.

– And why was that a bad thing?

Him needed ketchup.

101

Hooman!! HOOMAN!!!

    – Yes Indy?

Butler, me fink me is broked. Help.

    – Well, what did you do.

Me wuz havin mum cootches...

    – It's Cwtch.

Yeh... me not Welsh though is me?

    – OK, so you were cuddling mum.

Yeh an den head went like dis an me is stuck.

    – You mean you're just trying to get to the shortbread in the polar bear.

Well... yeh... a bit.

    – I swear mate if you break my DeLorean... or the Lego tie fighter...

Me not! Me is stuck. Butler help!

    – Stop trying to nick food then you bin diving gipper.

Butler, dis is last warning. Cat is laffin. Cat say head is on backwards and cat gone to get old priest and young priest and den chuck me down sum stairs.

    – Mate, you haven't even seen The Exorcist.

No but cat have cos cat is demon from hell.

    – Well that is true at least.

Butler help!

    – OK.

An den buttle me some shortbread.

    – No, Indy.

Hooman!!

– Yes Indy?

Wot dis butler? Why dis here now?

– It's a 30mph sign Indy. We walk past it every day,
sometimes twice.

No. It new butler. Me bark.

– It's not new. It was there yesterday and the day
before and before that.

No butler. It new. Me bark. An bark an bark an bark an
bark an bark an bark an bark an bark an bark.

– Brilliant. You know, because I've got all day for this.

An bark an bark an bark an bark an bark

– Right... I'll just get a book out for a bit then shall I?
War and Peace perhaps? The entire collected works of
Terry Pratchett maybe?

An bark an bark an bark an bark an bark an bark...an den....

– You done?

An bark...

– OK, that's a no then...

...an den me do dat griffin fing. Me do dat for a bit...Gruff.
Gruff gruff gruff.

– Here we go... you'll get it in a minute...

An..... me sniff...

– And here it comes....

Me sniff... and... dis is da one me see before!!!

– Yes. And you know what that means?

Wot dat mean?

– It means you're an idiot.

Hooman...

– Yes Indy?

What butler doin?

– Me and Sam are playing Cobra Paw.

Wot dat?

– It's a game where you roll dice, match the symbols and have to strike fast and first to get it right.

Me play.

– OK you can play against Sam.

Wot me do?

– Roll the dice.

Dat mean me pick up box.

– No, it means...

Me pick up box an run away. Den me chuck box and do barking.

– No... that's not how to play.

Yeh, dat is. Den me get tuggy an den me summon butler an den me play tuggy.

– But that's not Cobra Paw.

It in new edition.

– No it's not, you're just fed up that we're playing and you feel left out.

Yeh... dat... an...an

– And it's got a cat on the box.

Yeh. Dat. Cat game. Dat not for butler.

Hooman!!

    – Yes Indy... oh no no no!!

Yeh... me is doing dis butler.

    – No Indy, you mustn't dig up the garden.

Me is doin dat butler. Butler should not have been on talkie phone.

    – Why?!? I mean, just... why?

Me seen Deep Impact so me is dat now. Me make bunker to hide in.

    – But that was a massive asteroid that was going to strike the earth.

Yeh. An first fing dat happen wuz it rain a lot. It been rainin butler.

    – Yes but... oh mate your mum is going to freak.

Why dat den? She be saved too. She in first... den me, den Sam, den cat, den you.

    – But the garden is her favourite thing

No... me is favrit fing. Den Sam, den cat, den you.

    – Well, I guess so but...hang on, why am I last?!

Cos you is just a butler. Mum first, den Sam cos him licky, den cat so me got sumfin to eat, den you... if dere is room.

    – At least I get a place I suppose.

Yeh... if you is a good butler and you buttle good.

    – She's still going to freak at you.

No. She freak at you cos me is handsome and you is just a butler.

Hooman...

- *Yes Indy?*

Why is you sad?

- *How do you know I'm sad Indy?*

Me dog. Me know. Me always know.

- *Well, Sam was with us for a week and he's gone back to his mum's now.*

Yeh. Me miss him too. Him come back though?

- *Of course. We're lucky like that.*

Den why you sad?

- *OK... well... what's the worst thing you can think of?*

Huh. Dat Peasy easy. Da B word.

- *Right... well imagine the worst thing you can think of happening to you every 2 weeks for years and years. Saying goodbye just rips my heart out every single time and it's never once gotten any easier.*

Yeh. Me can see dat.

Where mum?

- *She's on a night shift.*

So, it just me an you den butler?

- *For tonight, yes.*

Wot dat?

- *Ice cream.*

Wot dat?

- *A pint of guinness.*

An wot dat?

- *You've got treats and pawsecco, I've got ice cream and Guinness.*

Butler...

- *Yes Indy?*

Is you Bridget Jones?

- *Well.... maybe.*

Butler better not do hooman howling to music, cos you is not all by self butler, me is wiv you.

- *Yes. Yes you are. And the cat.*

Yeh, but cat not bovvered. You better not wear mum's big pants and slide down fire pole is all me saying.

- *OK Indy... Indy?*

Yeh butler?

- *Thanks mate.*

Heh... dis wot doggies do best butler, dis wot doggies do best.

Hooman!!

    – Yes Indy?

Wot dis movie on now?

    – This? This my friend is Raiders of the
    Lost Ark.

An me is named after dat hooman, butler?

    – Yes... please don't spoil this one.

But...

    – Oh God... OK what?

Him stoopid.

    – You better be able to back that up Indy,
    or it's crate time..

Ha!! Him stoopid. Him run away from ball.
Ball is for chasin.

    – Great. So you'd just chase the giant ball and
    let the nazis get the ark then would you?

Yeh. Dey get it anyway, open it an all dead.
Me just go later an pick up da ark.

    – Thanks Indy. Thanks a bunch.

Hooman!

   – Yes Indy?

Where is me butler?

   – Um... what?

Ha! Butler not know where me is. None hoomans know where me is. Me is in stealth mode.

   – Um... OK... what?

Dis for super-secret undercover operation steal cat food.

   – ...and this works how?

If me no see butler, butler no see me.

   – That's not how it works mate and besides, all you've done there is step on your blanket and got confused.

Yeh.. and know wot dat mean butler?

   – No?

Me is goin deep under covers!!!

   – Good grief.

Pahahahahahahha!!! Butler, point me in direction of cat food.

   – No Indy.

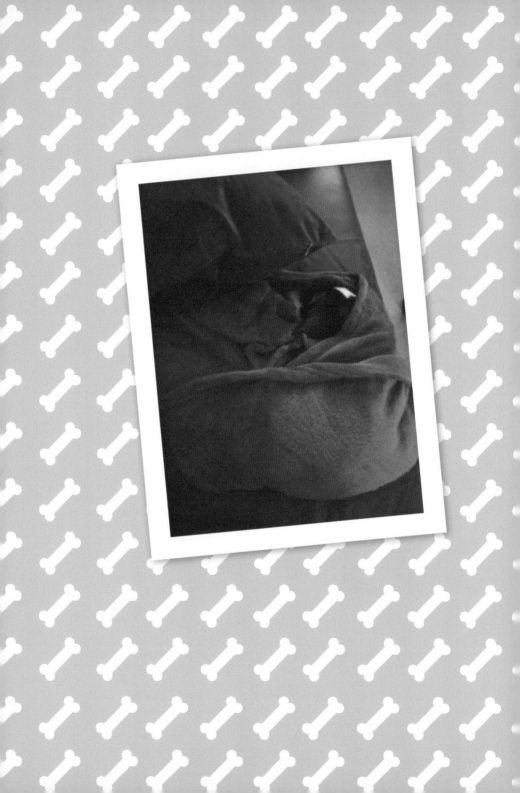

Hooman!

    – *Yes Indy... what are you doing?*

Dis is trap butler.

    – *A trap. And you've been caught have you?*

No, dis is trap for cat. Me lie in wait.

    – *Well, no, it's you in your blanket.*

Yeh, but dat is now. Wen butler have finished den it a trap

    – *Right.... OK so what do you want me to do?*

Butler get rope, cat food, cat box, boat hook, pulley system, paint an box of dynamite.

    – *Well... no, but...why?*

Butler tie me up in blanket and use rope an pulley so me hang over cat food. Den butler paint cat door on wall. Wen cat eat food, me drop down and cat go "meet meep" an try to run froo cat door and go blammo into wall. Den me catch cat wen cat is wobblin about.

    – *Right... have you been watching*
    Road Runner cartoons?

Yeh. Me is dat now.

    – *Well, what about the dynamite?*

Me need sumfin to do wen me has catched cat.

    – *No... just, no.*

Hooman!

　　 – Yes Indy.

Wot doin?

　　 – You know what we're doing. Having breakfast and watching
　　　 Spongebob... why have you got your innocent face on?

Nuffin...

　　 – What have you done?

NUFFIN.

　　 – Indy. You look guilty as anything, what have you done.

Butler left laptop on...

　　 – So? The network is locked down...wait... it's still on ebay...

Yeh... me goin out now.

　　 – No... you wait there.

Me goin out....um... need wee or sumfin

　　 – STAY. WAIT. GOOD BOY

Dat not fair butler.

　　 – Right. Let me see that... Oh God Indy, YOU SOLD THE CAT
　　 ON EBAY!!!! YOU SOLD THE CAT ON EBAY!!!!!!

Yeh... we need walkie to post office.

　　 – NO INDY! You cannot sell the cat!

But... it to nice hooman in Australia..hot dere and cat love it.
Dey got massive bouncey chickie.

　　 – You mean Kangaroo, yes they do don't they... anyway, no.

But me has already made cat in box ready

　　 – Go and get her out, now.

Bulter is spoiling sport.

　　 – NOW INDY!

OK butler. Me goin.

119

Hooman!

   – *Yes Indy?*

Look wot mum doin to trees!

   – *Yes, she's just cutting them back so they can grow again.*

Wot dat butler? Wot mum got dere?

   – *It's a little hedge trimmer.*

Me bite it. Like me bite hair dryer.

   – *No, I wouldn't do that mate.*

Me do jumping and bark an bark an bark an bark den.

   – *And what will that achieve?*

Me not know, but me do it anyway. Butler...?

   – *Yes?*

Cat is gettin more furry.

   – *No.*

Yeh, she very furry dese days.

   – *You're not hedge trimming the cat Indy.*

Yeh me is... oooh... me know, wot bout chainsaw?

   – *No.*

Yeh... butler get me chainsaw an hockey mask.

   – *No Indy, you're not chain sawing the cat.*

Yeh, me is.

Hooman!

– Yes Indy?

Look wot me finded on Octopus Prime.

– Amazon Prime and you're not allowed the TV
control after the Tom and Jerry incident...

But butler, it Titanic 2, dere is anuvver best film ever made.

– Indy, honestly mate it won't be any good. I mean the first
one was a bit pants.

Butler no say dat! Me love Jack an Rose best, best except mum.

– Yes, I know but Jack and Rose won't be in this one.

No Rose? No good boy best boy Jack?

– Well, look, it's set 100 years after Titanic.

Dats... dats...

– 700 years to you.

Dat is long time.

– Yes. So Jack and Rose won't be in it. Not unless it's
icy and they need something to grit the pavement with.

So why it called dat den?

– Well so as people will be fooled into watching it.
But when they do, they regret it.

Dat like wen cat is doin happy rumblin and den gets da finger knives out and is hissin. An stoopid hooman goes all kissy licky anyway.

– Um.... yes... a bit I suppose.

Hoomans is stoopid.

– Well... can't argue with that.

Hooman!

　　– Yes Indy?

Butler, me wants to play tuggy wiv Eaorle.

　　– No Indy, Eaorle was very expensive and he's OK
　　where he is.

Him not tuggy toy den?

　　– No, he's a muppet.

Ha, dat wot mum say you is butler.

　　– Funny. Very funny. Well thanks to you both mum
and　　　　　　　　　*Sam now call me butler too.*

Yeh. Cos dat wot me pay you for. You buttle.

　　– Right.. well, anyway, Eaorle is a Muppet.

Wot is Muppet butler?

　　– I'll show you... see? A hand operated puppe...

Butler wot you do wiv you paw in him bum?

　　– Well... I have to put my hand there to make him
　　speak, see.

Dat cool. Can me have muppet?

　　– No, I'd worry that you would just rip him, sorry.

Me want muppet.

　　– No, but we can make one for you.

Yeh. Me got idea.

　　– No.

Yeh. Butler get...

　　– NO.

Butler get cat and...

　　– No Indy you're not putting your paw up the cat.

Yeh me is... me bet cat eyes go all buggy like Muppet.

　　– No Indy, just... no.

125

Hooman!

– Yes Indy?

Get me chocklit, butler.

– No. Chocolate is bad for you.

No. It not. It bad for you if me no get sum.

– Um... are you threatening me?

OK... bad for cat den.

– Still no, no chocolates.

Dats it. No more Mr. Nice Doggy. Gimmie choc.

– Nope.

Right den. Me take chocklit tin. Ha! Dat fooled you, stoopid butler

– We'll see shall we?

Hey butler!!

– Yes...?

Dis tinm empty!

– Yep.

Dat not fair!!

– Well don't beg and then steal things when you get told no then.

Is choccies bad for cat?

– Actually I don't know. Probably.

Me can find out

– No Indy.

Me not give cat chocklit?

– No... of course not.

Marsy bar?

– No.

Twixt Two choc?

– No!!

Hokay. Butler get cat an me get double decker bus.

– No Indy, dear God no.

Hooman!

    – Yes Indy?

Look wot me found!

    – No no no!! That's mum's headwarmer!

    That's not a tuggy toy!

Yeh, is now.

    – I'm taking it off you.

Nope.

    – Yes. Give it to me.

No. Me do gruffin fing... ready?

    – GIVE IT HERE

Nope... grrrrruff.

    – Right, don't make me pull it.

Mine. It mine.

    – STOP PULLING IT!!

Nope. Me not pullin it, butler is.

    – STOP!!

Butler?

    – Yes?

Me told you it tuggy toy.

    – But... but...damn.

Hooman!

   – Yes Indy?

Butler, me seen Jumanji movie.

   – OK....and?

Me is da Rock now.

   – But... you don't really look like... I mean..

Me is doin da eyebrow fing. Me is da Rock.

   – That's your ear. I mean, it's good and all,
   I've never seen a dog do that with one ear
   before, but it's not your eyebrow.

Well yeh.. cos me is dog, stoopid butler.

Dog eyebrow not move like dat. So me use ear.

   – Right... so you're The Rock then?

Yep. An dat mean...

   – No Indy.

Yep me is top world woofwoof champion.

   – It's not woofwoof it's WWF and he doesn't
   do that anymore.

Yeh, me do. Butler get cat.

   – Indy you are not piledriving the cat.

Yeh, me is.

Hooman!

– Yes Indy?

If me is in trouble butler, den why is you laffin?

– Because it's hard not to laugh.

Wot me done bad?

– Well, you tell me what you did...

Hokay. Me was on walkie.

– Yes, a nice walk up to the town.

Yeh an me was good boy best boy and dint walk in road or nuffin.

– Yes. Your lead walking is going great...
but then what?

Well... den me sees dis anuvver doggie

– Yes... carry on...

An him was ickle small yapper terrorist.

– Terrier. Yorkshire Terrier. Not terrorist...
but yes

An me went an said hello.

– Yes.

An den me did wee on him.

– Pahahahahahaha!!!

Wot wring wiv dat!?

– You did a wee on his head!! I had to
apologise to his mum and everything.
Good job she laughed really.

Yeh, dat bad innit.

– I'm telling the cat Indy.

No butler, just no.

Hooman!

   – Yes Indy?

Butler, me got dis. Dis mine now.

   – Good grief Indy no, look at the size of it!

Yeh. Big innit. Dis favrit stick.

   – That's not a stick. That's a freakin tree mate.

Mine.

   – No.

Yeh. Dis mine stick. Dere is many like it but dis is mine. No stick, me is nuffin. No me, stick is nuffin.

   – Indy, this is not Full Metal Jacket.

Yeh is an dis coming home wiv me.

   – And what exactly will you do with that then?

Me seen 300. Me is Spartan now and dis is spear.

   – No it isn't.

Yeh, is. Me fight cat in glorious battle. Butler paint me six-pack wen doin tummy tickle.

   – No. Anyway, she's not a Persian cat.

   She's a tabby.

Dat better, dey not so cross, just hissin an spittin an finger knives.

   – OK, let's see how far you get.

Butler, carry dis spear.

   – No Indy. Just, no. You're not fighting the cat with a spear.

Yeh me is.

135

Hooman!

> – *Yes Indy?*

Butler, get box. Me found squeak chickie.

> – *Mouse. It's mouse. And no.*

Yeh. Me needs to catched squeak chickie.

> – *Why? What do you need a mouse for?*

Me got plan.

> – *Oh God... what?*

Cat chase squeak chickie yeh?

> – *Well, more that she rips them to pieces and leaves*
> *bits of them on the floor... but yes.*

Yeh, dat. An squeak chickie run zoomin fast away from cat...

> – *Well.... yes I suppose some of them must.*

So me stick squeak chickie to cat an...

> – *This sounds like the toast plan...that didn't work out*
> *so well for the cat...*

Yeh, dat.

> – *OK...and then what?*

An den cat go zooming round an round an gettin faster an
faster an den...

> – *Wait... you're saying that the cat and the mouse*
> *will create an infinite energy loop that will solve the*
> *discrepancy between Einstein's special relativity and*
> *quantum mechanics, thus creating the first true*
> *perpetual motion and solving the world's energy crisis*
> *and enabling future travel to other worlds.. essentially*
> *the long sought-after warp drive?*

Yeh, dat.

> – *Wow... I mean... that could work I guess.*

Yeh. An den cat explode.

> – *Oh, well, no then.*

Yeh...me get squeak chickie, butler get cat and staple gun.

> – *No, Indy.*

137

Hooman!

    – Yes Indy... how did you get that scar on your nose Indy?

Dat? Dat Voldemort.

    – Really. You sure it's not where you ran hell for leather after a deer and ran straight into a hedge because you're an idiot?

Nope. Me seen Harry Potter so me is dat now. Dis is scar an dis is wand.

    – Right... not just a stick then.

Nope. Dis wand. Fourteen inches, flexibubble and cat tail core.

    – OK...

Me goin to Dogwarts.

    – I really don't think...

Yeh me is. Me learn spell. Avocado Cadaver Cat.

    – It's Avada Kadavra and, well, no.

Yeh. Accio Cat.

    – Right.... and is the cat flying through the air yet?

No but me not been Dogwarts yet. But me can levitate cat. Me can do dat.

    – And how will you do that?

Butler get me robes.

    – Ok...

An hat,

    – OK.

An glasses.

    – OK...then what?

Den me throw cat off roof.

    – No, Indy.

Hooman!

    – Yes Indy?

Me need to get on roof of shed.

    – Well...no. It's not safe.

Ha!! Me no care for safe butler, me seen Daredevil so me is dat now.

    – Daredevil...

Yeh, dat me.

    – You're Matt Murdock, blind and with enhanced
    sensory abilities, even echo location and the ultimate
    in balance and control with unparalleled gymnastic and
    martial arts skills across multiple disciplines.

Yeh. Dat me.

    – And you want to get on the shed?

Yeh. Me do sneakin and lie in wait for cat who is Kingpin crime boss.

    – Are you quite sure you're Daredevil?

Yeh... dat me butler.

    – Only, you just walked into a chair. You've just wrapped
    your blanket around your head is all.

Me is Daredevil butler.

    – So... if you're Daredevil, why do you need me to get you
    on the shed? Can't you just do some awesome parkour
    up to the roof?

Yeh... me can do dat... but...

    – But what?

Me can no open door.

    – You're an idiot.

141

Hooman!!!

    – Yes Indy?

Wot dat butler?!

    – That my friend is a Nerf ball cannon.

    You want the ball?

Yeh yeh yeh yeh me want ball now now now....

    – Ready?

Yeh wot it do?

    – It fires the ball like this!

Wowowowowowowoowowowowow!!!

That awesome!!!!!

    – Yep.

Butler...

    – Yes?

Dat ball...

    – ....yes...

It bout same size as cat's head.

    – No...just no.

Hooman!

    – Yes Indy?

Butler me seen Ocean's Elephant now so me is dat now.

    – Ocean's Eleven Indy...

Yeh, me keep finking elephant turn up in movie but him dint turn up.

    – Anyway...so?

Me steal dese biccies.

    – I don't think so Indy. We can see you.

Yeh, me know dat. Me will pull a clever boy good boy con and den rob da casino of biccies.

    – OK... so what's the plan?

Nuffin... butler not worry bout dat...BUTLER QUICK!! OVER DERE IS A BADGER ON MOTORBIKE AND WIV A GUN!! LOOK!!

    – No Indy.

Oh. Dat not work den?

    – Nope. That was the worst con in the history of the world.

Yeh.. me fink of anuvver plan den. Me fold cat up in tiny box and send into biccie cupboard.

    – No.

Yeh. Me fold cat up. Cat get biccies.

    – If I give you a biscuit, will you leave the cat alone?

Yeh, me do dat

    – Right, have a biscuit then...

Fanx. Butler?

    – Yes Indy?

Me got biccie!! Dat was best con ever. Me is Ocean's Elephant now.

    – But... but.. damn.

Hooman!

– Yes Indy?

Play game wiv me butler.

– OK... how about Scrabble? Labyrinth? Cobra Paw?

No. Me want to play wot me is.

– Oh God, not again.

Yeh. Dis. Dis is me, an you guess wot me is.

– Titanic. It's always Titanic.

Nope. It not movie or howlin, or book.

– It better not be the one where you are a chocolate Mr Whippy machine because that was disgusting and we don't do that on the carpet.

No, not dat. Me sorry bout dat. Wot me is?

– Give me a clue.

Me is hooman. Me is butler's favrit howling hooman wot is not Kylie

– James Hetfield. Corey Taylor.

Nope. Look at me! Big clue... wwoooooooowowowowoow-ooowoooowee... an den butler do same fing...

– Oh God no... Freddie Mercury.

Yeh, dat.

– You know that the movie Bohemian Rhapsody was almost entirely made up and was wrong from start to finish?

Yeh.. me know... but... butler build Wembley Stadium in garden and me do Live Aid.

– No.

Butler can be Roger Taylor..

– Oh... OK then. Just don't tell the cat.

147

Hooman!

- *Yes Indy?*

Butler, me is building.

- *Um... OK... what?*

Me seen Doctor Mental on TV...

- *What? What are you talking about?*

It all about French Revlution. Was good. Me like. Me see dis on Sky Doctor Mental.

- *Ah.. Documentary. Sky Documentary.*

Yeh, dat.

- *Well, at least you're not just watching movies all the time... anyway... good was it then?*

Yeh... dem peeple hoomans was revolting.

- *You mean they revolted.*

Yeh, dat. An wen dey was revolting dey dint eat cake like good boy best boy, dey had fight wiv Mario an Luigi.

- *Good grief, you mean Marie and Louis. Marie Antoinette and Louis 14th... not Mario and Luigi.*

Yeh... dem. Was good. Dey give me idea

- *So.. what are you building?*

Me find dis wood.

- *Yes, and?*

Butler get cat. Me build guillotine.

- *No, Indy, just no.*

149

Hooman!

– Yes Indy?

Butler, look at dat! Me found Sparkle Chickie!

– Well, we call it a Peacock. Be careful, they can be aggressive.

Yeh but she very pretty.

– Well... that's a male.

But dat too pretty.

– Even so, that's the male. They have all these beautiful colours and they do this huge fan thing with their tail feathers.

Dat cool. Me like dat. Dat like Kylie dancing hoomans.

– Yes... yes, I suppose it is in a way.

Butler, get me sparkle collar an sparkle coat cos me is dat now.

– You want to be a Peacock?

Yeh. Me is dat now.

– OK... one problem, I mean, you can be anything you want, but Peacocks don't eat chicken.

No chickie?

– Nope, or beef.

No moo chickie? Not even sossij?

– No. Just grubs and seeds really.

Den me just be me

– Sounds good.

But weekends me be fabulous and sparkle.

– Good for you mate, good for you.

Hooman!

    – Yes Indy?

Butler get me out of dis. Me is stucked.

    – Right... well what were you doing?

Me seen Predator so me is dat now...

    – Yes... and?

Me saw it, over dere, past dem trees an me fink me no got time to bleed so me did chasin...

    – After a Predator?

Well...yeh.

    – Not a squirrel.

Nope. Not squiggle. PREDATOR.

    – And how do you know it was a Predator?

Cos me not see it. Stoopid butler.

    – OK, good point. Then what happened?

Den me fell in, did da mud fing on face and now me is stuck.

    – You're an idiot.

Butler quick, it got bomb on its fitbit.

    – Come on, let's go home. Spongebob is on Netflix.

OK but butler get me ole painless mini-gun..

    – No.

Me get to da chopper?

    – Whatever gets us home Dutch.

Yeh... can me watch Predator 2?

    – For the love of God, no Indy.

Hooman!

– *Yes Indy... what do you want.*

Butler not be cross. Dis sorry face me doin.

– *No. No. You're still laughing.*

Me is only laffin cos it funny. Me is sorry reeeeeeeeeealy.

– *Why? Go on then... explain yourself.*

Well...butler took me walkie. Cos you is butler an dat wot butler do. Dat wot me pay you for. An you is good at dat

– *Hmmm.... stop flattering me, it won't work... carry on.*

An butler, me went to park an me did good boy best boy zoomin and runnin an chasin an zoomin..

– *Yes, and you stopped at every road too, so that was good.*

Yeh, cos me is good boy best boy.

– *Yes, well don't push it...*

Den me stop cos me needed do chocklit Mr. Whippy.

– *Yes...yes you did.*

An den, wen me done chocklit Mr. Whippy, butler bent down an pick up chocklit Mr. Whippy...

– *Yes?*

Me did da stand still moonwalk fing wot dogs do and kick da chocklit Mr. Whippy over butler.

– *Stop laughing. It's not funny.*

Yeh is. Me IS sorry, but it still funny.

Hooman!

    – Yes Indy... wait...what are you doing?

Nuffin, butler not see nuffin. Be on your way.

    – No. No I don't think so... what are you up to?

Me said. Nuffin. Me no do nuffin.

    – Look, no one sits there with their ear to the sofa.

Me do. Me can... um... yeh, me can hear da sea.

    – No you can't, that's sea shells. What are you doing?

Me is just... listnin.

    – What for... wait... where's the cat?

Um...cat upatairs, sleepin.

    – No she isn't. I've just been upstairs and she's
    not there.

Den...den...cat gone out. Um....cat gone to roller disco.

    – No... that's Tuesdays. Have you stuffed her in
    the sofa?

No!

    – Indy...

Well, yeh. A bit.

    – A Bit?! You've stuffed the cat in the sofa... a bit?!

Yeh... a lot den.

    – Get her out.

Cat like it in dere.

    – No, she doesn't.

Dat wot me listnin at. Cat laffin. Well... a bit.

    – Just get her out Indy.

Hooman!

    – Yes Indy?

Is dis some sort of sick cat joke, butler?

    – What's that mate?

In dis ball, dere is anuvver.

    – Another what?

Anuvver ball butler. Look... dere.

    – But...Indy, that's the ball.

No... dat WAS ball... an den me chew off furry ball and me find anuvver ball. Dat not fair.

    – No... look... it's a tennis ball and they're covered in a kind of felt, that's all.

No butler. Dis big news. Dis need widdlin on lamp-posts so doggies know bout anuvver ball.

    – Indy, it's not a conspiracy, that's just how balls are made.

Yeh, you say dat... but wot if, right, wot if inside cat is anuvver cat an anuvver cat...for ever an ever...an it all just cat all da way down?

    – OK... look at it this way, what's inside you?

Dat peasy easy. Dat is biccies an treats.

    – ...right...so inside the cat is...?

Hissin an spittin an finger knives an anuvver cat.

    – Well... you're not opening up the cat just because a ball gave you an existential crisis.

Yeh me is.

Hooman!

– Yes Indy?

Me found dis hidden valley butler. Me seen Kong Skull Island so me is dat now.

– It's a runoff channel from an abandoned water mill.

Nope. It valley into lost world wiv diner saw, and tuggy toy kong.

– Dinosaur, you mean Dinosaur... And it's King Kong, or just Kong.

Dat wot tuggy toy is.

– Different Kong Indy. Anyway, what would you do if you found Kong down there?

Play tuggy, stooped butler.

– Mate... Kong is not a tuggy toy. He's a 300-foot-high silverback Gorilla with a fixation for blonde ladies and swatting aeroplanes out of the sky.

OK den, me got plan butler.

– No. We're just going home.

Yeh... butler me stay here. Me lookout for Kong Tuggy Toy... butler get cat, remote control plane and lots of sellotape.

– No Indy, just no.

Hooman!

   – Yes Indy... OK what are you doing?

Me is doing filthy dancing butler.

   – Please God, no...and it's dirty, not filthy.

Me seen Dirty Dancing so me is dat now.
Dis is cha cha cha.

   – They didn't do the cha cha cha in that Indy,
   they mainly did variations on a tango and a quick
   step I think.

Wotever dey did, me do it bestest.

   – Indy... you do know that movie is about a 35 year
   old man seducing and grooming a 15 year old girl right?

No say dat butler.

   – But Indy... it's just wrong. No one seems to care
   about that but it's just so very wrong.

Butler stop barkin. Butler not spoil it just cos it not Star
Wars or Wolverine wot mum want to lick face. Bad
butler, no biscuits.

   – OK, I'm sorry.

Butler, just for dat, you do lift fing.

   – No

Yeh. Me run zoomin an jump an butler lift me up.

   – No

Yeh... and butler put on sparkle pants too.

   – Well... OK... but you can't tell the cat.

Dat OK... me have superglued cat in da corner.

   – Nobody superglues the cat in a corner.

Me do. Me having time of life.

Hooman...
- *Yes Indy?*
Wot dat?
- *That's our little rainbow maker. Me and Sam bought it for mum.*
Wot it for?
- *It makes a rainbow.*
Yeh. Dat pretty. All dem pretty greys. Me like da grey one bestest.
- *We use it when we want to be closer to Penny, but you probably think that's silly.*
No, me get dat. Me can sniff Penny here.
- *Yeah, she was a good dog and we miss her all the time.*
It OK. Doggies is never gone for uvver doggies cos we do sniffin fing.
- *Yes, although I suppose it must be weird for you being able to catch her scent around the house.*
No. It nice. It make me waggy.

- *Well, humans need to think that when we go, we go over the rainbow bridge and she's there waiting for us. For you too, come to think of it.*
Dat like in Thor. Me like dat. Mum want to lick him face too.
- *Not quite the same... just... a place where we'll all meet up again.*
Even cat?
- *Yes Indy, even the cat.*
Dat nice.
- *Awww mate...see, I knew you love the cat really.*
It good dat cat be dere. It mean me have sumfin to eat while me wait for you.
- *Do you really mean that?*
Well... no... course not. Me luv you butler.
- *Love you too Indy.*
Butler...?
- *Yes Indy?*
Don't tell cat.
- *OK.*

165

Printed in Great Britain
by Amazon